W9-BVM-130

DATE DUE

AUG 0 8 2000			

"I'll get it!" Katie Lynn shouted.

She grabbed the receiver, hoping it was her grandmother. "Hello?"

"Is this the Katie Lynn Cookie Company?" a strange voice asked.

What?

Was this some kind of joke? "Is that you, Tina?"

"No. This is Jason Chesterfield. I'm the owner of Chesterfield's Restaurant. I'd like to put in an order for cookies. Is there someone there who can help me?"

Katie Lynn had to sit down before she could answer. "Uh, well, yes, I guess that's me."

To Ruth, my "twin connection"—
and to
Gwen and Charles and James and Tambye,
with all my love

Text copyright © 1999 by G. E. Stanley.
Illustrations copyright © 1999 by Linda Dockey Graves.
All rights reserved under International and Pan-American Copyright
Conventions. Published in the United States of America by Random House,
Inc., New York, and simultaneously in Canada by Random House of Canada
Limited, Toronto.

www.randomhouse.com/kids

Library of Congress Cataloging-in-Publication Data:
Stanley, George Edward.
The Secret Ingredient / by G. E. Stanley ;
illustrated by Linda Dockey Graves.
  p. cm. — (The Katie Lynn Cookie Company; 1)
"A Stepping Stone Book."
Summary: At first Katie Lynn is excited when people start buying the
walnut chocolate chunk oatmeal cookies she is baking with her
grandmother's secret recipe, but then things get terribly complicated.
ISBN 0-679-89220-6 (trade). — ISBN 0-679-99220-0 (lib. bdg.)
[1. Cookies—Fiction. 2. Moneymaking projects—Fiction.
3. Grandmothers—Fiction.]
I. Graves, Linda Dockey, ill. II. Title. III. Series: Stanley, George Edward.
Katie Lynn Cookie Company: 1.
PZ7.S78694Se 1999 [Fic]—dc21 98-51569

Printed in the United States of America 10 9 8 7 6 5 4 3 2 1

A STEPPING STONE BOOK and colophon are trademarks of Random House, Inc.
THE KATIE LYNN COOKIE COMPANY is a trademark of Random House, Inc.
RANDOM HOUSE and colophon are registered trademarks of Random House, Inc.

The
Katie Lynn
Cookie
Company

#1

The
Secret
Ingredient

by G. E. Stanley

illustrated by Linda Dockey Graves

A STEPPING STONE BOOK™

Random House 🏠 New York

Contents

The Secret Ingredient

Chapter One

Grandma's Cookies

"I am *so* hungry," Tina said. "Do you have anything to eat in your house?"

Katie Lynn chuckled. "Are you serious? You know what an awful cook my mom is. My dad always throws away the leftovers when she's not looking."

"But I'm starving to death, Katie Lynn! I forgot to eat breakfast this morning." Tina paused. "Is there anything your mom *didn't* cook?"

"Well, maybe we can find something." Katie Lynn stopped the porch swing with her bare feet. "Come on. Let's go look."

Katie Lynn led the way to the pantry.

"Wow! I've never seen so many cans of soup before!" Tina cried. "Who eats them all?"

"My dad. After my mom goes to bed."

"Hey! Wait a sec! There's a bag of cookies up there—on the top shelf."

Katie Lynn looked up. "I think we've had those since Christmas."

"Who cares," Tina said, climbing up onto the counter.

Tina handed the bag of cookies to Katie Lynn. "Let's take them up to your room."

When the girls got upstairs, they both went for the big beanbag. Tina won, so Katie Lynn flopped on her bed.

Tina took a cookie out of the bag and stuffed it in her mouth. "Eww!" she said after a couple of chews. "It's kind of dry." She threw a cookie to Katie Lynn. "Taste one."

Katie Lynn ducked. The cookie hit the wall and crumbled onto the carpet. Katie Lynn picked up the pieces and threw them at Tina.

"War!" Tina shouted, jumping to her feet. She started hurling cookies, one after the other.

"Stop it! Stop it!" Katie Lynn cried. She covered her head and started giggling.

Finally, there were no more cookies in the bag. But there *were* cookie pieces all over the room.

Katie Lynn looked around. "What a mess!"

"Those cookies were awful," said Tina. "Now I have a bad taste in my mouth. And I'm still hungry." Tina's stomach made a gurgling sound.

Katie Lynn laughed.

"It's not funny," Tina said. But soon she was laughing, too.

Katie Lynn sighed. "I wish my grandmother was here. She makes great cookies." Just thinking about her grandmother's cookies made her mouth water.

Tina rolled over and looked out the window. "I feel like we've been out of school for a hundred years. It's so boring around here. There's nothing to do."

"If Jonathan Wilbarger were here, we could go to his house," Katie Lynn said. "But he's on vacation. He won't be back for a week."

"We'll be gone for a week, too," Tina said. "My dad said we're going to the lake again this summer. Are you going anywhere?"

Katie Lynn thought for a minute. "Florida. To see my grandma. I'll get a vacation and some of my grandma's cookies, too!"

Her parents hadn't actually told her they were going to Florida that summer. But Katie Lynn was sure they would like the idea. Her mother was always saying, "I wish your grandmother could see you now!"

"In fact, I'm going to get a head start on packing," Katie Lynn said. She stood up. "If you want, you can stay and help."

Chapter Two

The Trip to Florida

"I wish we were going to Florida, too," Tina said sadly. "I'm tired of that dumb old lake."

Katie Lynn frowned. "Really? I thought you liked it there."

"I do. But we go every summer," Tina explained. "And I've never been to Florida before."

"Tina! I have a great idea! Why don't you come with us?"

Tina frowned. "Do you think your parents would let me?"

"Of course they will!" Katie Lynn said. "You're my best friend!"

Katie Lynn started taking clothes out of her closet. "I can't wait for you to meet my grandma. You'll love her."

"I don't know about your grandmother, but those cookies sure sound good." Tina

headed toward the door. "I better go pack, too. Call you later."

Katie Lynn started cleaning up cookie crumbs. When she was finished, she went downstairs. Her parents were in the living room, talking in low voices.

"Mom, where are the suitcases?"

Mrs. Cooke grinned. "Why do you need a suitcase, dear? Are you planning to run away?"

"Don't be silly, Mom. I'm packing for my trip to Grandma's."

Her parents gave each other a look.

"I don't think we can go to Grandma's this summer," Mr. Cooke said. "I may be busy."

"That's okay, Dad. You and Mom don't have to go. Tina's going with me."

Her father sighed. "I don't think so,

Katie Lynn. The truth is, we can't afford it." Mr. Cooke picked up the newspaper and pretended to read.

Katie Lynn didn't know what to say.

Suddenly, a great idea popped into her head. She ran back upstairs, grabbed her piggy bank, and shook all of the money onto her bed. She counted her change twice. Seventy-five cents!

Well, that certainly wasn't going to buy a plane ticket to Florida.

She threw herself across her bed. How could she make enough money to go to Florida? There just had to be a way.

Katie Lynn snuggled up against her stuffed animals. She thought and thought. But nothing came to her.

It didn't look like she was going to Grandma's, after all. How was she going to break it to Tina?

"Katie Lynn?"

Mr. Cooke was standing in her doorway. He looked excited about something. "Your mother and I have a surprise for you."

"You do?" Katie Lynn cried. She scrambled to her feet. Maybe they'd changed their minds about the trip!

Before he could answer, Mr. Cooke scrunched up his nose. "What's that smell?" he asked.

Katie Lynn sniffed. "Dad, I think it's…smoke!"

Chapter Three

I Can Do It!

"It's coming from the kitchen!" Katie Lynn shouted as they raced downstairs.

"Oh, no! Not again!" her father cried.

They burst into the smoke-filled kitchen.

"Kathy?" Mr. Cooke called through the haze. "Are you in there?"

Mrs. Cooke coughed a couple of times. "Yes!" she gasped. "But I think we need to call the fire department right away!"

As she dialed 911, Katie Lynn heard sirens approaching.

Somebody started banging on the front door.

Katie Lynn ran to answer it.

"I saw smoke coming out your kitchen window!" explained Mrs. Merchison. "I knew your mother was trying to cook again, so I called the fire department."

Suddenly, two firefighters dashed through the front door.

"The fire's in the—" Katie Lynn began.

"We remember where to go," one of the firefighters interrupted her. "Same as last week, right?"

"Oh, if only your poor mother would let me teach her how to cook," Mrs. Merchison said.

Katie Lynn tried not to laugh. Mrs.

Merchison's cooking was even worse than her mother's.

"Just a little smoke damage," one of the firefighters said as he came out of the kitchen. "Everything is fine."

"Tell your mother to call me anytime," Mrs. Merchison said. "I'll come over with all of my cookbooks."

"I'll tell her, Mrs. Merchison," Katie Lynn promised. "Thank you!"

The firefighter gave Mrs. Merchison a funny look. "Didn't we put out a fire in *your* kitchen yesterday?"

Mrs. Merchison blushed and scurried out the door. Laughing, the firefighters followed close behind.

Katie Lynn started to close the front door, but the smell was so bad she left it open.

Just then, she saw her mother going upstairs.

"Are you all right, Mom?" Katie Lynn asked.

"Of course I am, dear. But I wanted to surprise you with some cookies—just like your grandmother's. I wanted to make up for the trip to Florida. I'm so sorry I burned them."

"Oh, that's okay, Mom," Katie Lynn said. "You don't have to bake anything for me. Really."

Just then, the telephone rang.

"If it's for me, I can't talk right now," Mrs. Cooke said. "I need to take a shower to get rid of this smoky smell."

Katie Lynn ran to answer it. "Cooke residence."

"Katie Lynn! It's so good to hear your

voice! I miss you so much!"

"Grandma! I've been thinking about you and your cookies all day! I wish I had some of them right now." Katie Lynn glanced around and lowered her voice to a whisper. "Mom just tried to bake some, but it didn't work out."

"Katie Lynn, if you want cookies, you should bake some yourself."

"Me? Are you serious, Grandma?"

"You've seen me do it a million times, dear. Weren't you paying attention?"

"Well, yes, but…"

"Then I'm sure you can do it. Your mother has all of my recipes in her recipe box. You know, the gray metal thing covered with dust?"

"I guess I could try, Grandma."

"That's my girl. Just do yourself a

favor—keep your mother out of the kitchen!"

"Don't worry. I will."

"Speaking of your mother, is she there?"

"She can't talk now, Grandma."

"Then just tell her I called and I'll talk to her later."

After Katie Lynn hung up, she punched in Tina's number.

"I can't go to Florida," she explained. "Don't tell anyone, but my parents said we can't afford it this summer."

"That's okay. Don't worry about it. Maybe we'll get to go next summer."

"Maybe," said Katie Lynn. "The good news is, I just talked to Grandma. She said I should try to bake some of her cookies myself. So I think I'll try today."

"Can I help?"

"Sure. My mom has all of her recipes. I'm going to bake my favorite kind first. Oatmeal Walnut Chocolate Chunk."

"Oh, wait a minute," Tina said. "I can't right now. I have to baby-sit my little brother all afternoon. How about tomorrow?"

Katie Lynn thought for a moment. "I have an idea. You can sleep over. Then we can get started first thing in the morning."

Chapter Four

The Secret Ingredient

"Rise and shine!" Katie Lynn sang.

Tina opened her eyes and groaned.

Katie Lynn peered at her watch. "It's four o'clock."

Tina yawned. "I can't believe we slept so late." She rolled over in her sleeping bag.

"It's four o'clock *in the morning*," Katie Lynn replied.

"*What?*" Tina cried. "Why did you wake me up so early?"

"Real bakers start at dawn," Katie Lynn said. "Besides, I want to surprise my mom and dad at breakfast."

"Cookies for breakfast?" Tina said. "Hmm. That actually sounds pretty good."

The girls made a beeline for the kitchen.

"First things first," said Katie Lynn. She read the ingredients for the Oatmeal Walnut Chocolate Chunk Cookie recipe out loud.

¾ cup vegetable shortening
1 cup brown sugar, firmly packed
½ cup granulated sugar
1 egg
¼ cup water
1 teaspoon vanilla

3 cups uncooked oats
1 cup all-purpose flour
1 teaspoon salt
½ teaspoon baking soda
1 cup walnuts
1 cup semi-sweet chocolate chunks

Tina took an egg out of the refrigerator and dropped it on the floor. Katie Lynn could tell that her friend was still half asleep. She searched the pantry for the rest of the ingredients.

"Believe it or not, we have everything," Katie Lynn said finally. "Grandma must have bought this stuff the last time she was here."

At that moment, Mrs. Cooke came into the kitchen. "What are you two doing down here so early?" she asked as she turned on the coffeemaker.

"We're baking some of Grandma's cookies," Katie Lynn explained.

Tina giggled. "Cookies for breakfast."

"Why are *you* up so early, Mom?"

"Your father and I couldn't sleep," Mrs. Cooke replied. "So I came down to make some coffee. I might as well stay and help you bake your cookies."

"No, really, Mrs. Cooke! You don't have to do that!" Tina turned to Katie Lynn. "We want to do it all by ourselves, don't we?"

Katie Lynn nodded. "It's very important that young people learn to be independent, Mom. We…uh…learned that in school last year."

"Well, okay. If you're *sure* you don't need my help. But don't forget the secret ingredient," Mrs. Cooke added.

Katie Lynn frowned. "Secret ingredient?" It sure wasn't written on the recipe card. She had no idea what her mother was talking about.

Mrs. Cooke opened the refrigerator. "I think it was something unusual. Something you wouldn't expect." She took out a bottle of ketchup and set it on the counter next to the ingredients. "Try this."

"I really don't think Grandma would put ketchup in her cookies, Mom." Katie Lynn put the bottle of ketchup back in the refrigerator.

"Well, you have to use the secret ingredient," her

mother said. "It's what makes your grand-mother's cookies so special. Call Grandma if you don't believe me."

Katie Lynn picked up the phone and punched in the numbers she knew by heart. Her spirit sank when the machine came on.

"Hi, Grandma, it's me. When you get this message, call me immediately. Mom says we're nowhere without the secret ingredient. I wish you were here!"

Katie Lynn hung up and turned to Tina. "Let's get started. Maybe she'll call back before we bake."

Shaking her head, Mrs. Cooke poured two cups of coffee and left the kitchen.

Katie Lynn rolled her eyes. "That was a close call." She finished reading the instructions, then turned on the oven to

350 degrees Fahrenheit. Tina got out the measuring cups, the measuring spoons, a mixing bowl, and a cookie sheet.

One by one, Katie Lynn measured out the shortening, brown sugar, granulated sugar, egg, water, and vanilla into the mixing bowl.

Tina beat everything together with a wire whisk until it was creamy.

Katie Lynn mixed in the oats, flour, salt, and baking soda.

Tina picked up the cup of walnuts, then put it back down. "Sorry, but I just don't like nuts."

"Then let's leave them out," Katie Lynn said. "All that really matters is the chocolate."

Suddenly, Mrs. Cooke appeared in the doorway. "I remember the secret ingredient!" She threw open the refrigerator door.

"It's pickle juice! I'm sure of it!"

Katie Lynn grabbed Tina's hand and squeezed hard.

Mrs. Cooke took a jar of pickles out of the refrigerator and set it on the counter. "It's a good thing I still have these from last summer." She poured two more cups of coffee and left the kitchen.

Katie Lynn put the jar of pickles back in the refrigerator. "Mom gets a little funny after too much coffee," she explained. "The secret ingredient is definitely *not* pickle juice."

Tina took a look for herself. "There's nothing else in here except a jar of mayonnaise. Do you think that's the secret ingredient?" Tina asked.

Katie Lynn shrugged. "Well, I know it's not ketchup or pickle juice." She glanced up at the kitchen clock. "If we want cookies for breakfast, we'll just have to take a chance."

Katie Lynn put a tablespoon of mayonnaise in the cookie dough. While she mixed it in, Tina greased the cookie sheet with a little vegetable shortening.

Then Katie Lynn scooped up six tablespoons of the dough and dropped them onto the cookie sheet. She put on an oven mitt and placed the cookie sheet on a rack in the oven.

Tina set the timer for fourteen minutes.

When it went off, Katie Lynn took the cookies out of the oven. She used a spatula to lift them off the sheet and put them on a platter.

"We have enough dough for about three more batches," said Tina.

Katie Lynn clapped her hands. "Let's go to it!"

After all of the cookies were baked, Katie

Lynn called out, "Mom! Dad! It's time for breakfast." She poured four glasses of milk and set a platter of cookies in the center of the table.

"These cookies are amazing!" her father said, taking a bite. "They taste just like your grandmother's."

Mrs. Cooke took a bite of cookie and closed her eyes. "I agree one hundred percent, dear."

Katie Lynn hoped her parents weren't just being nice.

"Our turn!" said Tina.

Katie Lynn didn't care if her mouth was full. "These *are* as good as Grandma's, Dad! It's a good thing we had the right secret ingredient!"

Outside, a car honked.

"Oh, no! That's my parents! I better get dressed!" Tina cried. "I almost forgot. We're going to Chesterfield's for lunch."

"Take some of the cookies with you," Katie Lynn said. "They're probably better than any dessert at Chesterfield's."

As Tina ran out the front door, Katie Lynn handed her a bag of cookies.

"I'll call you later!" Tina shouted over her shoulder.

Katie Lynn watched Tina and her family drive away. She wished that she and her parents were going to Chesterfield's for lunch, too. They had the best hamburgers in town.

When Katie Lynn returned to the kitchen, she found her parents still sitting at the kitchen table. But now the cookie platter was empty.

"What happened?" Katie Lynn cried.

Her parents looked embarrassed.

"We ate them," her mother admitted.

"They were just so delicious, we couldn't help ourselves," her father added.

Katie Lynn beamed. She'd never felt so proud of herself.

She went back up to her room and lay down on the bed. She reached over to turn on the radio and snuggled with her stuffed animals.

She was drifting off to sleep when the telephone rang.

"I'll get it!" Katie Lynn shouted, hoping it was her grandmother. She ran down the hall and grabbed the receiver. "Hello?"

"Is this the Katie Lynn Cookie Company?" a strange voice asked.

What? Was this some kind of joke? "Is that you, Tina?"

"No. This is Jason Chesterfield. I'm the owner of Chesterfield's Restaurant. I'd like to put in an order for cookies. Is there someone there who can help me?"

Katie Lynn had to sit down before she could answer. "Uh, well, yes, I guess that's me."

Real Money

Tina burst into Katie Lynn's room. "Did Mr. Chesterfield call?"

"I can't believe you! He wants six dozen cookies by tomorrow morning!"

Tina gasped. "Really? Did he tell you he's going to pay us?"

"You bet!" said Katie Lynn. "Now we can pay for our trip to Florida!"

"All right!" Tina cried.

Katie Lynn gave her friend a big smile. "It'll take a long time to bake all those cookies. You'll just have to sleep over again."

They ran to the living room to tell Katie Lynn's parents.

"It was all my idea," Tina claimed. "I told Mr. Chesterfield that we had a cookie company. The Katie Lynn Cookie Company," Tina added.

Katie Lynn felt her face turning red.

"Well, that's very exciting, but it's a lot of work, too," Mr. Cooke added. "And another thing...you'll need money to run a company."

"That's true. You'll have to buy more ingredients," Mrs. Cooke said. "I doubt we have enough ingredients left to make many more cookies."

"Oh," Katie Lynn said sadly.

"But I'll be glad to lend you two the money," her father said. "Of course, you'll have to pay me back out of the money you earn. That's the way it's done in business."

"We can do that, can't we, Tina?"

Tina nodded enthusiastically.

Katie Lynn got the recipe back out of

the box. It wasn't so dusty anymore. She made a list of the ingredients they needed. Then Mr. Cooke drove them to the grocery store.

One by one, the girls found all of the ingredients. By the time they were done, the shopping cart was piled high.

Mr. Cooke paid for everything. But

when they got back home, he handed Katie Lynn the receipt. "This is what you owe me," he told her.

Katie Lynn put the receipt in her pocket. "Okay. I'll pay you when Mr. Chesterfield pays us." She grabbed Tina's hand. "Come on! We have six dozen cookies to bake!"

"That's a lot of work for two people," Mrs. Cooke said. "Why don't you let me help you?"

Katie Lynn had to come up with an excuse—and fast!

Suddenly, she remembered how her parents had eaten the first batch of cookies.

"I know!" she cried. "You and Dad can be in charge of Quality Control!"

"*Quality Control?*" her father asked.

Katie Lynn nodded. "I heard about it on TV. We'll give you a cookie to eat from each batch we make. You get to decide if they're good enough to eat."

Mrs. Cooke smiled. "Oh, we can do that!"

Katie Lynn and Tina hurried out of the living room.

"Way to go!" Tina whispered.

Katie Lynn grinned and bowed. "Thank you! Thank you!"

The girls got busy baking cookies. By midnight, they were finally finished.

Mr. Chesterfield's cookies went into plastic sandwich bags. The girls made sure the bags were sealed super-tight.

"It's quitting time," said Tina. "I'm falling asleep on my feet."

"Sweet dreams about Florida," Katie

Lynn said as they tumbled into bed.

Tina yawned. "Are we going to fly coach or first class?"

"I think we should fly first class," Katie Lynn said. "People who own companies always fly first class."

The next morning, Katie Lynn's father woke them up.

"What time is it?" Tina groaned.

"It's time to take your cookies to Mr. Chesterfield. He just called. He needs them right away."

When they arrived at the restaurant, they found Mr. Chesterfield waiting impatiently. The girls rushed over to him with the bags of cookies, and Mr. Chesterfield gave Katie Lynn a check.

Mr. Chesterfield inhaled the aroma from the cookies. "Wonderful!" he

exclaimed. "In two days, I'll need twelve dozen more."

Tina grinned at Katie Lynn and said, "The Katie Lynn Cookie Company is up for the job!" Katie Lynn felt her face getting red again.

Their next stop was the bank. Mr. Cooke cashed their check and then gave them the money.

Katie Lynn paid her father for the ingredients. She split the rest of the money with Tina.

"You'll need to buy twice as many ingredients this time," Mr. Cooke said. "You'll need to spend part of what you've earned."

Tina frowned.

"What's wrong?" Katie Lynn whispered.

"We'll never save enough money for the

trip if we have to spend it all on ingredients."

"Yes, we will," Katie Lynn replied. "Even if it takes us all summer to save up!"

Chapter Six

Time Out!

One day at the bank, Katie Lynn whispered, "I've been keeping track, Tina. We have enough money for the trip now. Our hard work has paid off."

"Finally!" Tina said. "It's almost time for school to start and I don't even have a tan!"

When they got to her house, Katie Lynn remembered something important. "We have to tell our customers that we're going on vacation for a week."

They called Mr. Chesterfield first. He got very upset. "What do you mean?" he shouted. "My customers won't eat any of my other desserts! And Doris Goodworthy needs you to cater her next party!"

Doris Goodworthy? Katie Lynn thought. *The Mayor of Bakersville!*

"Of course, you could just let me have your recipe," Mr. Chesterfield went on, "and we could bake them right here at the restaurant. That way, you don't have to go on baking day and night when you get back."

Katie Lynn blinked in surprise. "We could never just give you the recipe, Mr. Chesterfield."

"No way!" Tina shouted into the phone.

"It's a Katie Lynn Cookie Company secret!"

"Oh, I wasn't suggesting that you *give* it to me. I'd be more than happy to pay for it."

Tina looked as if she was about to faint.

Katie Lynn took a deep breath. "We will be open for business when we get back."

After she hung up the phone, Katie Lynn felt horrible. "We're letting down all of our clients."

"It's our own fault," Tina said. "We bit off more than we could chew."

"We only started selling them to pay for our trip," Katie Lynn said. "I'm sorry Mr. Chesterfield is mad at us, but I want to see Grandma!"

"Then that's what we're going to do," Tina declared.

"Let's tell my parents first," Katie Lynn suggested.

They found Mrs. Cooke in the living room.

"Mom, Tina and I made enough money selling cookies for us to go to Florida," Katie Lynn said.

Her mother looked up. "Us? Just you and me? Oh, Katie Lynn! That's wonderful." She stood up. "Grandma will be so happy to see us! I can't believe we get to go to Florida after all!"

Katie Lynn gulped. She leaned over and whispered to Tina, "I think we have to talk."

"When I said *us*, I meant you and me," Katie Lynn said when they reached her room. "Mom thought I was talking about me and *her*. What am I going to do? You

saw her yourself. She was so excited. There's no way I could go without her now."

Tina sniffed. "You and your mom should be the ones to go to Florida. It was fun baking together. We can always go during Christmas vacation if we work hard this fall."

Katie Lynn felt her eyes fill with tears. "You'd do that for me?" she said.

Tina smiled. "Of course I would. You're my best friend. You always will be, no matter what."

After Tina left, Katie Lynn filled the tub for a bubble bath. Something was bothering her. She didn't feel good about her talk with Tina.

Tina had spent the whole summer baking cookies. She'd worked hard—and now she deserved a vacation.

Katie Lynn sighed. Why was life so complicated?

She climbed in the tub and sank into the bubbles. "If Mom and I go see Grandma, then Tina is stuck here. If Tina and I go to Florida, Mom will have to stay home. How can I see Grandma and still make everybody happy?"

It came to her while she was putting on her pajamas. The perfect solution. And she wouldn't have to use Tina's money, either!

Chapter Seven

Grandma's Big Surprise

"Why are you baking cookies so early in the morning, Katie Lynn?" her mother asked as she turned on the coffeemaker. "You should still be in bed."

"I don't have time to sleep, Mom," Katie Lynn said. "Tina's baby-sitting Gerald this morning, so it'll take me twice as long to get the orders done without her."

Mrs. Cooke gave Katie Lynn a big hug.

"I can hardly wait to go to Florida." Then she poured two cups of coffee and left the kitchen.

The doorbell rang just as the oven timer dinged. Katie Lynn heard her mother opening the front door. She grabbed an oven mitt and took the cookies out of the oven.

Suddenly, her mother screamed, "Mother!"

Katie Lynn ran into the living room and shouted, "Surprise, Mom! I used the money to fly Grandma here to see us!"

"Oh, Katie Lynn!" her mother said, clapping her hands. "You're so thoughtful!"

Mr. Cooke had come downstairs to see

what all the commotion was about.

"Breakfast is served!" announced Katie Lynn. She placed a pitcher of milk and a platter of freshly baked cookies on the table.

When her parents went upstairs to get dressed, Katie Lynn joined her grandmother in the kitchen.

"We did it, didn't we, Grandma?" Katie Lynn said.

"We certainly did." Her grandmother picked up a cookie and started nibbling on it. "Katie Lynn, these are much better than mine. What's your secret ingredient?"

Katie Lynn hesitated. "Mayonnaise," she said finally. "What's yours?"

"Cream cheese," her grandmother replied. "But I think I like mayonnaise better." She gave Katie Lynn a pat on the shoulder. "No wonder your company is doing so well."

"That's the problem," Katie Lynn said.

"What do you mean?"

"I don't know what to do, Grandma. I don't think Tina and I can do all of this baking once we start school. Our customers really count on us."

"Hmm. That *is* a problem. Speaking of problems, I have one, too."

"What is it, Grandma? Is everything okay?"

"The truth is, I'm really not very happy in Florida. I miss you and your parents so much. What would you think if I moved in here and helped you with your cookie company?"

"Oh, Grandma! That would be so incredible!"

"I know we'd have great fun, but I worry about how your parents would feel."

Mrs. Cooke stuck her head in the door. "Your dad and I will be right back."

"Just a second," said Katie Lynn. "Mom and Dad, someone you know very well wants to come live with us. She's very unhappy where she is right now."

"Tina wants to move in with us?" her mother exclaimed.

"No, Mom! I'm not talking about Tina," Katie Lynn said. "I'm talking about Grandma."

"Grandma!" her parents cried.

"If I lived here, I could bake cookies while Katie Lynn and Tina are in school," her grandmother said. "It'd bring in some extra money, and we'd all get to be together."

Mr. Cooke looked pale.

"Mom, I think we should…" Mrs. Cooke began.

Just then, Tina rushed into the kitchen. "Please tell me that we have to bake cookies today!" she said. "If we do, I can stay instead of having to baby-sit."

"We do have to bake cookies," Katie Lynn said.

"Phew," Tina sighed.

"We also need to have a company meeting," Katie Lynn added.

Tina hopped up on the counter. "What's up?"

"I'd like to introduce you to my grandmother. She's going to move in and help us bake cookies," Katie Lynn said.

"All right!" Tina cried.

Mr. Cooke headed out of the room. "I

think I'll mow the lawn," he said with a grin. "No need for me to attend company meetings."

Mrs. Cooke sat down at the table. "Since we're in charge of Quality Control, I'd better stay."

Katie Lynn saw her grandmother raise an eyebrow. "It's a long story, Grandma," she whispered, stifling a giggle. "We'll tell you *all* about it at our next sleepover!"

What's Katie Lynn cooking up next?

Book #2
Frogs' Legs for Dinner?

Three's a crowd in the kitchen...

"I need to start dinner," Mrs. Cooke announced.

"Oh, Kathy! We can't leave the kitchen now," said Grandma. "We have one more batch of cookies to bake."

"There's no need to leave the kitchen," said Mrs. Cooke. "We can all work in here together. It'll be fun."

Katie Lynn didn't think it would be fun at all, but she didn't say a word. How long would it take her mother to drop the French chef act?

Mrs. Cooke began to prepare the snails for cooking. Katie Lynn tried not to look at her future dinner.

Suddenly, Grandma screamed, "There's a snail in my cookie dough!"

ABOUT THE AUTHOR

G. E. STANLEY has written over fifty books for young people, several of them award winners. He and his wife, Gwen, live in Lawton, Oklahoma. They have two sons, James and Charles, and a Labrador retriever named Daisy.

"When I'm not writing books for young people, I'm in our kitchen baking cookies for my family," says G. E. Stanley. "Some of my favorite secret ingredients are carrot juice and mashed potatoes." Thinking about this gave him the idea for *The Secret Ingredient*. "I've never sold any of my cookies the way Katie Lynn and Tina do. But I've certainly given away lots of them for holiday gifts."

ABOUT THE ILLUSTRATOR

LINDA DOCKEY GRAVES grew up in New England, drawing and painting both plants and people. She moved to California, where she received a degree in illustration from San Jose State University. Now Mrs. Graves lives in southeastern Virginia with her husband, two sons, and a menagerie of pets. She has illustrated over twenty books for children, including *The Enchanted Gardening Book*.

#1 *Kidnapped at Birth?*

"Wonderfully logical and absurd, with a wit and attention to detail rare in an easy reader...Sachar has a rare honesty about what children really encounter in the world."

—*The Bulletin of the Center for Children's Books*

#2 *Why Pick on Me?*

"Vintage Sachar—ingenious, funny, gross—and with a believable resolution."

—*Kirkus Reviews*

"A tour de force of the genre, a trim tome of energy, hilarity, and wisdom...It will be an underground classic, an easy reader that kids are dying to read."

—*The Bulletin of the Center for Children's Books*

...by award-winning Louis Sachar!

#3 *Is He a Girl?*

"Sachar writes for beginning readers with a comic simplicity that is never banal. Kids will love the frankness."

—Booklist

#4 *Alone in His Teacher's House*

"The usual hilarious comedy...[but] the story takes a surprising turn."

—Booklist

#5 *Class President*

"This easygoing and humorous adventure confirms Marvin as a staunch friend of the intermediate reader."

—The Bulletin of the Center for Children's Books

Don't miss

Marvin Redpost #1:
Kidnapped at Birth?

"Mr. and Mrs. Redpost," he said. "I have something important to tell you."

"Mr. and Mrs. Redpost?" asked Mrs. Redpost.

He took a breath. He wasn't quite sure how to say it.

"Marvin Redpost is dead," said Marvin.

Don't miss

Marvin Redpost #2:
Why Pick on Me?

Marvin felt terrible. In fifty years they'll dig up the time capsule. And they'll find out a boy named Marvin Redpost picked his nose. And everyone will laugh at him.

Maybe in fifty years he'd be president! But then they'd dig up the time capsule and say, "You can't be president anymore. You picked your nose."

It wasn't fair.

Don't miss
Marvin Redpost #3:
Is He a Girl?

Marvin waved the bat back and forth.

He was afraid of Clarence but tried not to show it.

Suddenly Clarence laughed.

Then everyone else laughed too.

The umpire spoke to Marvin. "I'm sorry, young man," he said. "But you can't play. You're out of uniform."

"Huh?" asked Marvin.

He looked down at his clothes. He was wearing a dress.

Don't miss

Marvin Redpost #4:

Alone in His Teacher's House

"Marvin, may I talk to you for a moment?" asked Mrs. North.

He walked to her desk.

"Do you like dogs?" asked Mrs. North.

"Sure," he said.

"I'm going to need someone to take care of my dog Waldo while I'm away," said Mrs. North.

Marvin could hardly believe his ears.

"I'll pay you three dollars a day," said Mrs. North. "I'll give you a four-dollar bonus if there are no problems."

Marvin nodded his head. He was too shocked to speak.

Don't miss
Marvin Redpost #5:
Class President

Mrs. North looked lost.

"Are you all right?" asked Kenny.

"We are going to have a visitor today," Mrs. North said finally.

Marvin couldn't wait to hear who it was. From the way Mrs. North was acting, he thought it must be somebody weird.

"Who is it?" asked Warren.

"Is it somebody I've heard of?" asked Nick.

"Oh, I hope so, Nick," said Mrs. North. Then she took a deep breath and said, "The president will be coming here."